RON WEGEN

Sky Dragon

Greenwillow Books, New York

Library of Congress Cataloging in Publication Data

Wegen, Ronald.   Sky dragon.
Summary: The children look up at the snow-filled
clouds in the sky and see them as various animals
which give them an idea on what to build with the snow.
[1. Clouds—Fiction.   2. Snow—Fiction]   I. Title.
PZ7.W4233Sk   [E]   81-7219
ISBN 0-688-01144-6   AACR2
ISBN 0-688-01146-2 (lib. bdg.)

For Sean, Janis, and Althea

"My nose is cold."

"I see a dog."

"My hands are cold."

"Aren't those elephants?"

"Yes, but my ears are going to fall off."

"Wow!"

"I want hot chocolate."

"It's getting dark. We better go home."

"It's snowing."

"It snowed all night.
Let's build a snow fort."

"I've got a
better idea."